D1315533

THE WIND BEFORE IT BLOWS

By

Cynthia DiLaura Devore, M.D.

Published by Abdo & Daughters, 4940 Viking Drive Suite 622, Edina, Minnesota 55435.

Library bound edition distributed by Rockbottom Books, Pentagon Towers, P.O. Box 36036, Minneapolis, Minnesota 55435.

Edited by Julie Berg

LIBRARY OF CONGRESS CATALOGING-IN-PUBLICATION DATA

Devore, Cynthia DiLaura,1947-
    The wind before it blows / written by Cynthia DiLaura Devore.
       p. cm. -- (Children of courage)
    Summary: Turell discovers that the encouragement and support he received from his mother is a legacy passed from generation to generation. Includes how-to's.
    ISBN 1-56239-247-6
    [1. Self-esteem -- Fiction. 2. Parent and child -- Fiction. 3. Afro-Americans -- Fiction.] I. Title. II. Series: Devore, Cynthia DiLaura. 1947-   Children of courage.
    PZ7.D4993Wi   1993
    [Fic}--dc20

                      93-7723
                        CIP
                        AC

The loss of a family member creates a sadness shared by all—adults as well as children. The legacy left behind, however, can often help mitigate the family's loss, especially when that legacy is passed down from generation to generation. THE WIND BEFORE IT BLOWS takes a tender look at the marvelous formula for success a single mother gave her son—a formula which he will surely pass on to his son. Set in the inner city, the story creates an atmosphere of hope from despair. It imparts a strong sense of self-esteem to the young reader.

3

Every Tuesday, Turell Johnson and his mother took a walk to the park in his neighborhood. It was not a large park. In truth, it was not really a park by most people's standards. It had been a vacant lot, now cleared and cleaned. Over the years small trees were carefully planted by the community. This year some park benches and flower beds were added. Many people still referred to the park as the "Vacant Lot." Yet to Turell, it was "The Park" and his favorite place to go with his mother.

As they walked down the street on their way to The Park, Turell said to his mother, "Mama, last night I had a dream."

His mother touched his black curly hair softly and smiled. "I once knew a King who had a dream," she said. "Dream, Turell, dream."

They passed the corner grocer. They stopped as always
to buy a pretzel stick. They continued their trip and walked
past some boys who were huddled together against the
lamppost. His mother looked concerned and took Turell's
hand. He knew that meant they were kids he should avoid.
She always told him, "With friends, no explanation is
needed, and with enemies, no explanation will suffice. Stay
away from people who are not your friends, Turell, stay away
from people who can hurt you. Take care, Turell, take care."

They continued walking, past the store front church they attended together every Sunday morning. He often saw his mother smile as they passed the church. This must be her favorite place, he thought, just like The Park is my favorite place. How lucky they were to have their favorite places so close to their home.

"Mama, I dreamed I saw a rainbow in the dark," Turell told his mother. "Do you really think I can see rainbows in the dark?"

She smiled and said, "If you believe you can do something, Turell, then I believe you can too. Believe in yourself, Turell, believe in yourself."

They came to The Park. There were scattered puddles here and there from a light morning shower. The puddle water sparkled in the sunlight. The pinks and yellows and blues from the flowers were bright. He loved his park.

They walked to the sandbox. He sat next to his mother on the ledge of the box. She handed him an old spoon, a dented sifter and two small clean margarine tubs she had brought from home. He loved to dig with his toys and sift the sand.

"Mama," Turell said quietly, "I dreamed I felt the wind before it blew. No one else could. I was the only one."

She smiled again and said, "That's because you are so smart. You are the only you, Turell. No one can ever be you. Know that you are important, Turell, know it."

Turrell started to dig a hole with the spoon in the sand. The sand was just wet enough to be fun. His hands were grainy and the hole was a little well filled with water. He spooned water into the sifter and watched it drip.

"Mama, I am going to be a great scientist who makes an important discovery someday," he said.

His mother rose from the ledge and walked to the park
bench. It sat in the morning sun. He watched her as she sat
down. He thought she was the most beautiful mother there.
He was happy flowers had been planted on either side of
the bench, because it looked as if she were a queen on a
throne.

She said, "You can be whatever you want to be, honey. You
only need to study hard and learn well. Learn, Turell, learn."

Turell finished digging in the sand and walked to the swings. He called to his mother to push him.

"Push me high, Mama. Make me touch the white cloud with my toes. Help me to fly."

His mother came over to him. "You do it, Turell, all by yourself. Make yourself fly. Set your goals high and reach for them. Fly high, little bird, fly high. Fly away."

As years passed, trips to the park became fewer. He grew up remembering his mother's words. "Set your goals high and reach for them." He learned well. He came to believe in himself. He made careful, thoughtful choices.

Turell went to college and became a scientist. He married and had a son of his own. They visited Turell's mother often over the years.

One very sad day, Turrell's mother died. Turell returned to his mother's house to close it. He stood quietly watching as the movers emptied his mother's house of her furniture. He stood by the window looking out onto the street. He could see the church and The Park from his window, and he smiled.

"Our favorite places, Mama," he whispered to himself.

"Turell, Turell," his wife said. Startled, he turned to see his wife in the now empty room that was once filled with the love of his mother. "The mover would like to speak with you before he leaves."

The mover was standing next to his wife. "Yes, Dr. Johnson, we have loaded the last piece onto the truck. If you'll sign here, we'll be on our way," he said.

"Thank you for your help," Turell said.

"You're welcome," said the mover. "Good-bye." He tipped his hat to Mrs. Johnson and left.

"We're ready to lock up the house now," she said, pausing. "Are you okay Turell?" She took his hand. She knew how hard it had been for him to lose his beloved mother. Closing the house where he grew up was very painful for him.

"Yes," Turell sighed. "I was just remembering how much my mother gave me while she was alive. I didn't realize it at the time, but I am what I am because of my mother. This house isn't the same without her. Her things don't belong here any longer. I think she'd be happy to know we donated them to the Homeless Shelter." His wife smiled and nodded in reply.

Just then his son came running in. "Daddy, come look, they've put a new climbing set in Grandma's Park. Will you help me climb to the top? It's so high, I bet I could touch the clouds."

Turell bent down, took his son's hands and smiled, "Sure son, I'll come and watch, but you can do it all by yourself." Then he looked down and said in a low voice, "Fly high, little bird, fly high."

His son overheard the whisper. "Hey, that's what Grandma always used to say to me." His tone suddenly saddened, and he dropped his head. "I miss Grandma, Daddy," he said pausing. "A lot."

His father bent down and hugged the boy. "I know, son, I do too." They hugged in silence for a moment. This was a time when silence was more important than words. There were no words to describe the sadness they both shared over the death of their mother and grandmother.

Soon Turell broke the silence, "Now, how about you showing me that great new climbing set? Let's go play in Grandma's Park. You have some cloud touching to do."

The boy became excited and scampered down the steps. His mother followed. "Can we stop at the grocery store to buy a pretzel?" the boy asked.

"Good idea, son," he said as he lingered at the door.

"Come on, Daddy," his son called.

Turell was the last to walk out the door. "Coming," he reassured his son. He looked inside the darkened house one last time. "Thank you, Mama," he whispered. Then he closed the door.

How To Encourage Success

• Admire the child's accomplishments and encourage the child's pride in his or her own work.

• Help the child learn new ways of dealing with problems by anticipating what a situation may be like and how he or she might respond.

• Emotionally healthy children have a loving relationship with at least one adult during childhood.

• Children need to count on an adult to be there for them, to meet their physical needs, to protect them, and provide rules and structure.

• Don't minimize the need for academic success.

• Support areas of true strength. Help a child be an "expert" in some area.

• Express your unconditional love, love that is not based on performance.

• Establish traditions. Find one thing to do, one place to go, one song to sing, that is special.

About the Author:

Dr. Cynthia DiLaura Devore is a pediatrician with a strong interest in School Health and Education. Her role as a school physician makes optimal use of her training and experience in both education and medicine. She lives in New York with her husband and two sons.